# creation COLORS

## by Ann D. Koffsky

APPLES & HONEY PRESS

To Aaron, Jeremy, and Adira
for enriching my life with *nachas* and exhilarating colors.

And with thanks to Mandy
for showing me how to make a paper cut.

Apples & Honey Press
An imprint of Behrman House
Millburn, New Jersey 07041
www.applesandhoneypress.com

ISBN 978-1-68115-545-6

Library of Congress Cataloging-in-Publication Data

Names: Koffsky, Ann D., author, illustrator.
Title: Creation colors / by Ann D. Koffsky.
Description: Millburn, New Jersey : Apples & Honey Press, an imprint of
Behrman House, [2019] | Summary: Illustrations and easy-to-read text
portray the biblical story of Creation through colors God used each day.
Identifiers: LCCN 2018014186 | ISBN 9781681155456
Subjects: | CYAC: Creation--Fiction. | Color--Fiction.
Classification: LCC PZ7.K81935 Cre 2019 | DDC [E]--dc23 LC record available at https://lccn.loc.gov/2018014186

Design by Alexandra N. Segal
Edited by Dena Neusner
Printed in China

1 3 5 7 9 8 6 4 2

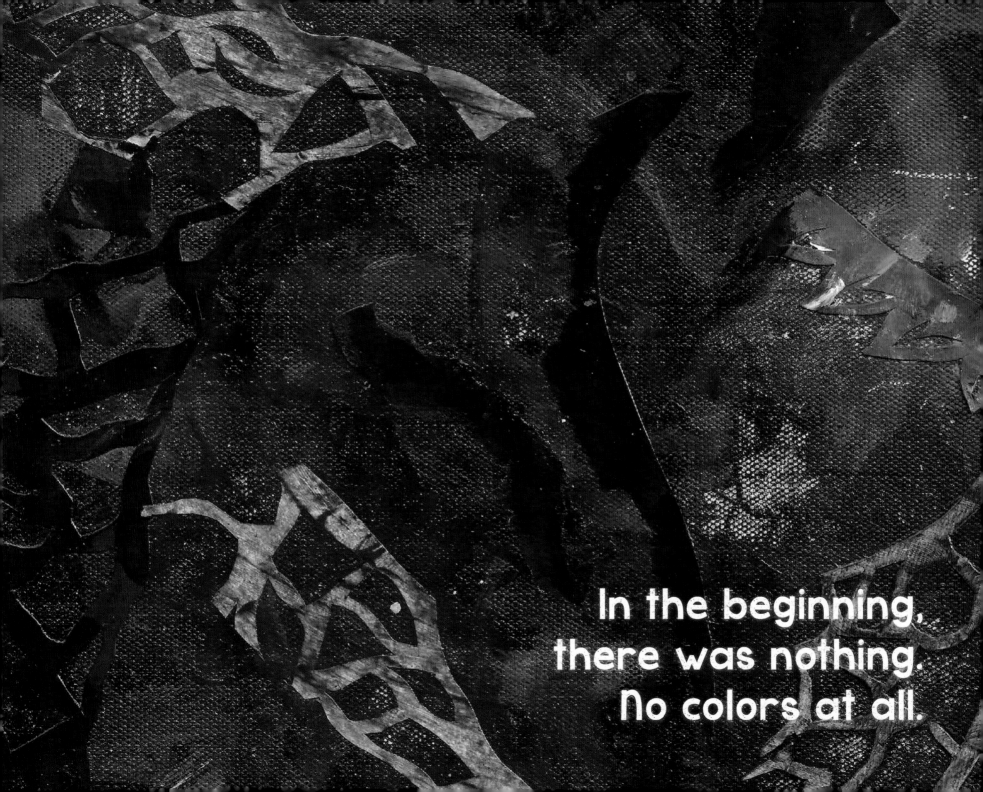

In the beginning,
there was nothing.
No colors at all.

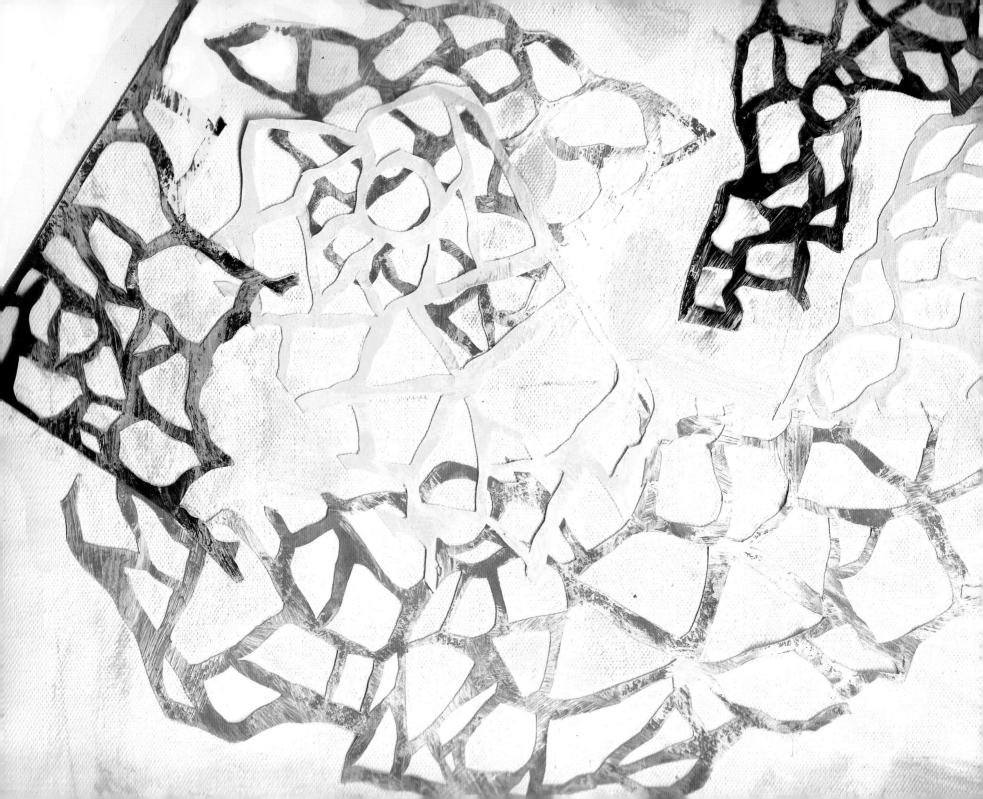

God had to make everything.
Even the colors. It took
six days to make them all.

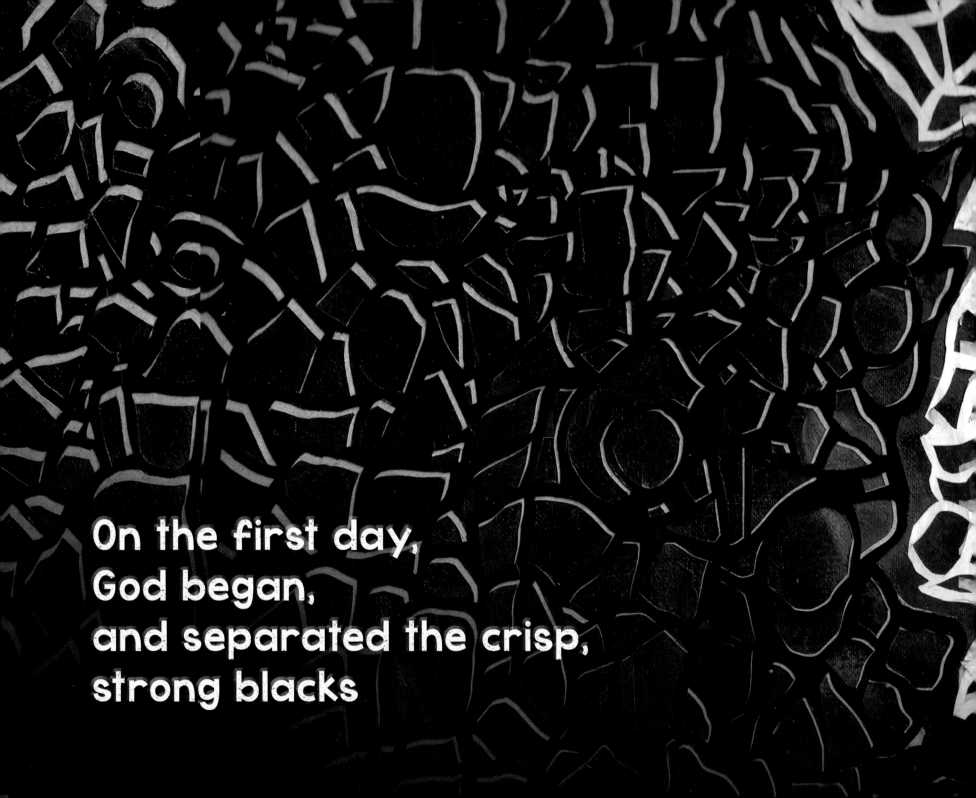

On the first day,
God began,
and separated the crisp,
strong blacks

from the wintry, pale whites.

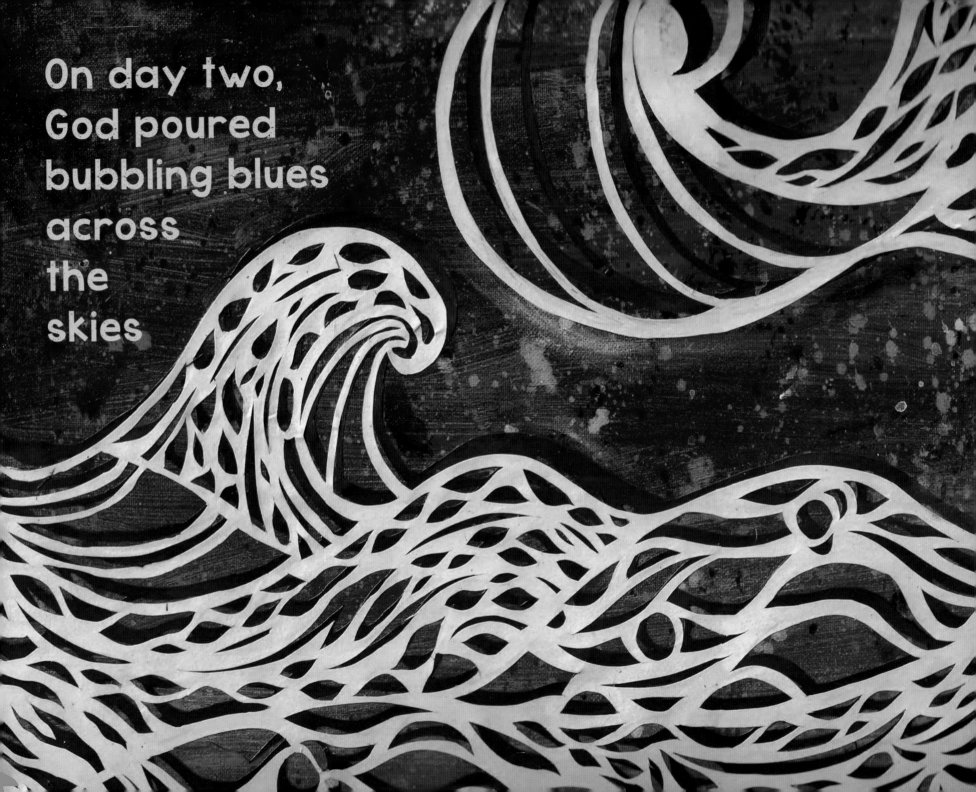

On day two,
God poured
bubbling blues
across
the
skies

and into the
watery oceans
and seas.

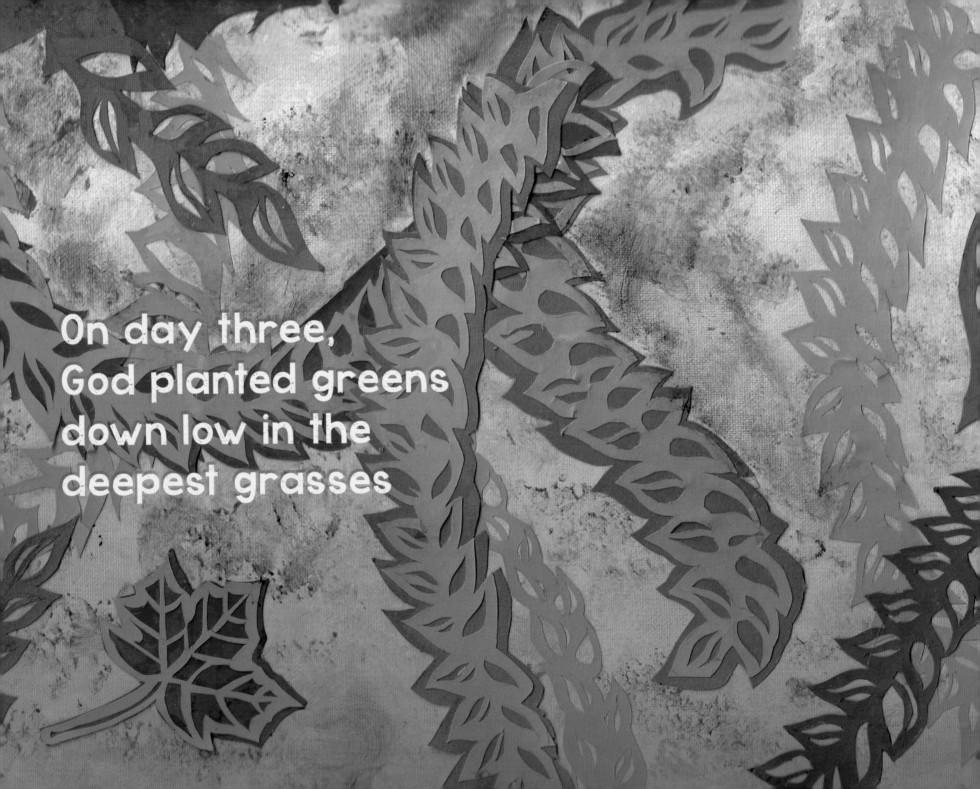

On day three,
God planted greens
down low in the
deepest grasses

and up high on the tallest trees.

On day
four, God lit
the skies

with burning yellows and oranges bright enough to shine through all the days and nights.

On day five, God made pinks that swam

and reds that flew too fast to catch.

On day six,
God created the animals.

They had stripes and dots, flecks and specks,

and dots, flecks and specks,

textures and patterns
of every kind.

And then it was time
for the people.
God started with
just two.

And God looked at all these creation colors and said,

"This is very good." And it was.

And on the seventh day, God rested.

Dear Readers,

COLOR is one of those things that we often take for granted. It is everywhere around us, and if it suddenly went away we would miss it terribly. (Can you imagine if the world was a colorless mush?) If we take the time to notice it, we can see how wonderful color can be.

The same is true of everything that God created in those first six days, according to the Bible:

**Day 1: Light and Dark**

Day 2: Sky and Waters

Day 3: Trees and Plants

**Day 4: Sun, Moon, and Stars**

**Day 5: Fish and Birds**

Day 6: Animals and People

**Day 7: Rest and Shabbat**

Maybe that's why the Bible shares all those details of Creation with us. It's to tell us, "Hey! See that sun? Imagine if it wasn't created! See those birds? That flower? Imagine if they weren't here. Don't think they are ordinary. They are *extraordinary!*"

Take a moment and look around you. What colors do you see? What things do you see that may look ordinary but are really extraordinary?

With warmth and color,

*Ann*